Good-bye Mommy

by
Bruce King Doman

Illustrated by
David Melton

The Better Baby Press

8801 Stenton Avenue
Philadelphia, Pennsylvania 19118
(215) 233-2050

For our boys, Erik and Shannon,
and my wife, Karen

This edition, Tenth Printing, 1985

Text: Copyright © By Bruce King Doman
Illustrations: Copyright © 1977 By David Melton

Format Design By Glenn Doman
Cover Design By David Melton
Printed in the United States of America

Library of Congress Catalog
Card Number: 77-79632

ISBN # 0-936676-00-0

Here is Tommy.

And here is

his Mommy.

His Mommy

is going,

And Tommy wants

to go, too.

But is she going

without him?

Tommy does not

know what to do.

But his Mommy

can not go

without saying

good-bye.

So Tommy

will hide.

Then his Mommy

will stay.

Tommy hides

in the closet,

but out creeps

his ear.

He hides

in the kitchen,

but out creeps

his nose.

He hides

in the bathroom,

but out creeps

his toes.

He hides

in the bedroom,

but out creeps

his head.

He hides

behind the chair,

but out creeps

his belly-button.

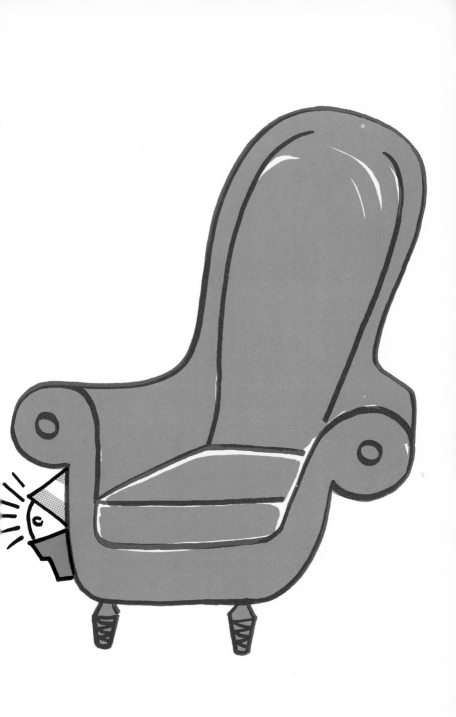

He hides

behind the table,

but out creeps

his hair.

He hides

behind the door,

but out creeps

his hand.

He hides

behind the T.V.,

but out creeps

his foot.

He hides

in his bed,

but here

he stays.

Now Mommy

is leaving.

But where

is Tommy?

He is not

under the chair.

He is not walking

with sister.

He is not reading

with Daddy.

He is not playing

with brother.

Mommy can not

find Tommy.

Sister can not

find Tommy.

Brother can not

find Tommy.

But Daddy can

find Tommy.

Tommy is hiding

in bed.

Now, Mommy

is laughing.

Tommy, I am going

to the zoo.

And I am

waiting for you.

The hippopotamus

is in the zoo.

The giraffe

is in the zoo.

The rhinoceros

is in the zoo, too.

Many animals

are in the zoo.

Your sister

is going.

Your brother

is going.

Your daddy

is going.

Do you want

to go, too?

ABOUT THE AUTHOR

Bruce King Doman was raised at The Institutes for the Achievement of Human Potential. He was, himself, a very early reader and at seven, raced his father, Glenn Doman, for the newspaper which he read from cover to cover. Today, he is an attorney-at-law and the Assistant Public Defender of Pennsylvania's Bucks County.

ABOUT THE ILLUSTRATOR

David Melton is one of the most versatile and prolific talents on the art and literary scenes today. His illustrations have been featured in many books and national magazines, and have been reproduced as posters, puzzles, calendars, book jackets, and record covers.

Mr. Melton's literary works span the gamut of factual prose, analytical essays, news reporting, magazine features, poetry and novels. His books include: TODD; I'LL SHOW YOU THE MORNING SUN; JUDY — A REMEMBRANCE; WHEN CHILDREN NEED HELP; THIS MAN, JESUS; BURN THE SCHOOLS, SAVE THE CHILDREN; CHILDREN OF DREAMS, CHILDREN OF HOPE; HAPPY BIRTHDAY AMERICA; A BOY CALLED HOPELESS; AND GOD CREATED; and HOW TO HELP YOUR PRESCHOOLER LEARN MORE, FASTER AND BETTER

Mr. Melton lives in the Midwest with his wife, Nancy, and their two children, Todd and Traci.